THE BIG MOVE

by Wendy M. Bretz

tate publishing

Published by Tate Publishing & Enterprises, LLC
127 E. Trade Center Terrace | Mustang, Oklahoma 73064 USA
1.888.361.9473 | www.tatepublishing.com

Tate Publishing is committed to excellence in the publishing industry. The company reflects the philosophy established by the founders, based on Psalm 68:11,
"The Lord gave the word and great was the company of those who published it."

Book design copyright © 2012 by Tate Publishing, LLC. All rights reserved.
Cover and interior design by Stan Perl
Illustrations by Justin Stier

Published in the United States of America
ISBN: 978-1-62024-438-8
Juvenile Fiction / Religious / Christian / People & Places
12.06.14

DEDICATION

For my husband, Joe, who encouraged me to pursue a creative outlet to declare God's glory.

ACKNOWLEDGMENTS

Thank you to Dave and Gloria Furman and Casey Pettett who gave honest feedback and told me to go for it. I'd also like to thank my parents for teaching me to pursue my dreams. Thank you to the Tate Publishing team who made my dream a reality.

Most importantly I want to thank my Savior Jesus Christ. His story is the best anyone can ever tell. I pray this book brings you glory, Lord.

"I don't want to move!"

"Timothy Walter Sherman," his mother said softly, "you should be happy for your father. It's been difficult for him to find work."

"Move, move, move," Lisa sang, clapping her hands together.

What does she know? She's not even two. She won't be the only kid who doesn't have anyone to play with. Timmy slouched in his chair. "Humph," he muttered.

After supper Timmy stomped into the living room. The doorbell rang. It was Timmy's grandfather. After exchanging a smile with Timmy's mother, he walked over to Timmy.

"Any room for me?" he asked gently.

"I guess so."

"Something on your mind?" Timmy shrugged. "So your father announced the big move. I take it you're not excited."

Timmy shrugged again.

"You know, Timmy, God has a plan for everyone's life. Sometimes God's plan includes things that we don't want to accept… like having to move away from friends. Is that it?"

"I'm happy here. I don't want to move away. Who will I play with?"

"You'll be surprised by what God has around the corner. This might seem like a difficult situation, but God is in the business of making a way when the way seems impossible."

"How do you know?"

"God told me."

"What do you mean?"

Timmy's grandfather picked up his Bible.

"Grandpa, that's a Bible. God talks to you through a book?"

Timmy's grandfather chuckled. "God doesn't talk to me like I'm talking with you. The Bible is a collection of stories that tells us God's plan throughout history from beginning to end. Along the way, God's people have faced impossible situations, and God made a way for them. This helps me to remember that he will do the same for me."

Timmy's grandfather turned to the book of Exodus and read about how God's chosen people—the Israelites—were slaves in Egypt.

"That's terrible. What happened to them?"

"God chose a man named Moses to lead them out of Egypt."

"They could just leave with this guy?"

"No, Tim. God had to bring ten plagues on the Egyptians before Pharaoh would let them go. Then Pharaoh changed his mind and chased the Israelites into the desert. The people were very scared. They had no weapons and nowhere to run or hide. The Red Sea was in front of them, and Pharaoh's army was coming behind them."

"Did they fight off the army with rocks and sticks?"

"They didn't have to. God placed a pillar of fire behind them to protect them from the army. Then, God opened the sea, and they passed through it on dry ground. When the Egyptians tried to follow, God closed the sea again and the army drowned."

"Wow! God did that?"

"He certainly did."

"Okay. God is able to save a bunch of people from an army. But does he care about just a few people like Dad, Mom, Lisa, and me?"

"I know a story about three young men who God saved from a fiery furnace." Timmy's grandfather turned to the book of Daniel and told him about Shadrach, Meshach, and Abednego—three young men who chose to stand up for God at the expense of their lives.

"These young men were ordered to worship the king instead of God. They refused, and the king became very angry. He decided that if they wouldn't bow down to him, they didn't deserve to live. He ordered them to be thrown into a furnace."

"That doesn't sound like a good thing…" Timmy said.

"No. The king had the furnace heated more than usual and had his soldiers throw them in."

"I thought you said God saved them!"

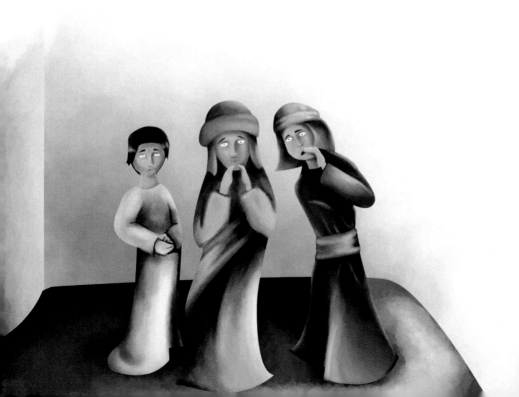

"He did! You didn't let me finish. The king was waiting to see the end of these young men, but do you know what he saw instead?"

"What?"

"He saw Shadrach, Meshach, and Abednego walking around in the fire unharmed with a fourth person who the king described as a son of the gods. This might have been an angel God sent to comfort these young men or even Jesus himself."

"That's impossible!"

"Nothing is impossible with God. When the king saw that they were not going to be harmed, he ordered them to be taken out. He declared that their God should never be spoken of badly or there would be severe consequences."

"So God cares about a few just like he cares about many. But these stories are about people so long ago. How can I know that God cares about me?"

"Do you know that God has numbered the hairs on your head?"

"Are you sure?"

"Yes, I'm sure. Jesus said so. Jesus also said that once you belong to God's family, you are safe in his hands, and no one can ever take you away from God."

"But I'm part of the Sherman family. How do I get into God's family?"

"John three sixteen in the Bible says, 'For God so loved the world, that he gave his only Son, that whoever believes in him should not perish but have eternal life.'"

"I've heard that before, but I don't understand it."

"Let me try to explain it to you. Remember when your dad announced the big move?"

"Yes."

"Remember how you reacted?"

"Yes."

"Why did you react that way?"

"Because I don't want to move," Timmy said quietly.

"How about what your parents want or what God wants for your family?"

"I didn't think about that."

"What were you thinking of?"

"Me," Timmy said, slumping his shoulders.

"So you agree that your behavior was selfish? You were only thinking about how this would affect you, right?" Timmy nodded his head. "Tim, do you know that you were born with a sinful nature?"

"What's that?"

"It's what Adam passed down to us when he and Eve disobeyed God in the garden of Eden. Do you remember that story?"

"The one with the apple and the snake?"

"That's the one. Because Adam disobeyed God by eating the fruit, mankind's relationship with God was broken. Every person who has been born since has been born with this sinful nature. We all want to do what's wrong instead of what's right. So, when you were only thinking of yourself, you were acting according to your sinful nature."

"Everybody has this?"

"Everyone." Timmy's grandfather paused and then asked, "Tim, do you know that acting selfishly is the opposite of acting with love?" Timmy thought for a moment and nodded his head. "Do you know that when we choose not to love others, we are actually sinning against God because we are breaking his law?"

"I never thought of it that way."

"Do you know why sin is a big deal?" Timmy shook his head. "Do you remember learning about why Jesus came?"

"To take away our sins."

"That's right. Jesus came to take the punishment for sin when he died on the cross and rose again. Our sin separates us from God because God is holy. He can't have sin in his presence. He has to punish sin because sin is wrong and he is good. He wouldn't be a good God if he let sin go unpunished. God placed all the punishment for our sin on Jesus. We don't have to be afraid of God or his judgment of our sin because Jesus already paid for it."

"But that doesn't answer how we get into God's family."

"Okay. Here it is. You need to admit to God that you have not acted the way he wants and believe that Jesus's death has paid for your sins. God will adopt you into his family, change your heart, and give you his Holy Spirit. The Holy Spirit helps you to choose what God wants instead of what your sinful nature wants."

"That's it?"

"That's it. A lot of people think they have to be good enough to earn God's forgiveness. But, Tim, none of us could do anything perfectly enough for God's standards. On top of that, none of us could erase the wrong we've already done. That's why we need Jesus. Jesus met God's standards and lived a life without any sin. He was able to die in your place because he didn't have any sin of his own.

You were right. Jesus came to take away your sin. But there's more to it than that. He will take your sin and give you his righteousness. That means when God looks at you, he doesn't see all the selfish things you've done. He sees all of Jesus's selfless actions instead. God will no longer see all the times you broke his law by failing to love others. He will see all the times Jesus kept his law and loved others perfectly. That's how God fixed our broken relationship."

"So that verse about God sending his Son…what did it say again?"

"John three sixteen says, 'For God so loved the world, that he gave his only Son, that whoever believes in him should not perish but have eternal life.'"

"Humph."

"A lot to think about, right?"

"That's for sure. God sent his Son to take the punishment for my sin because he loves me and wants to be with me, and all I have to do is believe it," answered Timmy.

Both Timmy and his grandfather were silent for a few moments gazing out the window.

"Can I get into God's family today?"

"You can get into God's family right here on this couch."

"I just have to say I'm sorry and that I believe?"

"Just talk to God about it."

"Dear God, I'd like to be part of your family. I know I've done things that have broken your law like how I acted at the table. I'm sorry I was selfish. I believe that you sent your Son Jesus to take the punishment for my sins. Thank you for loving me so much. Amen." Timmy looked up at his grand-father and saw tears in his eyes. "Are you okay?"

"Yes, Tim. I'm just so happy that you've put your faith in Jesus."

"Me, too."

"So if God can part a sea, keep people from burning in a furnace, and even take care of everything that kept you and him apart, do you think he can take care of you and your family when you move? Even bring you some new friends?"

"Yeah, Grandpa, he can."

"Of course he can. This doesn't mean it will be easy. It means that whatever life brings God will walk through it with you."

Timmy's grandfather gave him a squeeze and then put a stern look on his face. "Now," he said in a deep voice, "do you think you should apologize to your parents?"

Timmy giggled. "Okay." He hopped off the couch and walked swiftly to the kitchen. "Dad, Mom...I'm sorry for being selfish. I'm glad Dad got a job. I'll be sad to move, but Grandpa says God has a really great plan for us...and I believe him."

"Oh, Timmy, it's so good to hear you say that," his mother exclaimed, pulling Timmy into her arms. Timmy's dad came over and threw a bear hug around both of them. In the background, little Lisa continued the chant in her singsong voice, "Move, move, move!"

Timmy's grandfather sank into the couch and smiled.

e|LIVE

listen|imagine|view|experience

AUDIO BOOK DOWNLOAD INCLUDED WITH THIS BOOK!

In your hands you hold a complete digital entertainment package. In addition to the paper version, you receive a free download of the audio version of this book. Simply use the code listed below when visiting our website. Once downloaded to your computer, you can listen to the book through your computer's speakers, burn it to an audio CD or save the file to your portable music device (such as Apple's popular iPod) and listen on the go!

How to get your free audio book digital download:

1. Visit www.tatepublishing.com and click on the e|LIVE logo on the home page.
2. Enter the following coupon code:
   a937-08b6-7bef-9b99-6c34-0379-2066-2432
3. Download the audio book from your e|LIVE digital locker and begin enjoying your new digital entertainment package today!